P9-BZI-602

MARC BROWN

Arthur, It's Only Rock 'n' Roll

Little, Brown and Company
Boston New York London

For Laurie —
You're always rock 'n' roll to me

First Edition

Adapted from a teleplay by Kathy Waugh

Brown, Marc Tolon.
Arthur, it's only rock 'n' roll / Marc Brown — 1st ed.
p. cm.
Summary: Francine starts a rock band, hoping it will focus on music rather than money and fame.
ISBN 0-316-11854-0
[1. Musicians — Fiction. 2. Rock music — Fiction. 3. Animals — Fiction.] I. Title.
PZ7.B81618Anag 2002
[E] — dc21 2001050714

10 9 8 7 6 5 4 3 2 1

LAKE

Printed in the United States of America

Muffy was watching a Backstreet Boys video again.

"How can you watch those sellouts?" said Francine. "They don't care about music. They just want to make money."

"If you had a band," said Muffy, "you'd sell out in five minutes."

"If I had a band," said Francine, "it would be a million times better than the Backstreet Boys, and I'd *never* sell out!"

Muffy snorted. "Oh, yeah? Prove it!"

"I will!" Francine stormed out.

Everyone wanted to try out for Francine's new rock band, but auditions weren't going well. Francine had rejected everybody so far.

George came out of the music room, shaking his head sadly.

"Next!" shouted Francine.

"I can't believe I auditioned fourteen people and they all stank. Except for you, of course," said Francine.

"You know what they say, honey," Mrs. MacGrady said. "If the mountain won't come to Muhammad, then Muhammad must go to the mountain."

"Go to the mountain . . . hmmm," said Francine. "So, who are the best musicians we know?"

Francine went to Binky's house first.
"Will there be snacks?" Binky asked.
Francine nodded.
"Okay," said Binky, "I'm in."

Then Francine asked Molly and Fern to
join her band.

"Francine wanted *them* but not *us?*" said Buster.
He and Arthur couldn't believe it.

At the band's first rehearsal, Francine was very excited.
"Guess what!" she said. "Mr. Haney wants us to perform at the PTA fund-raiser!"

"But we don't even have a name yet," Molly said.

"We'll think of something," said Francine. "Let's play."

"Stop that noise!" yelled a neighbor. "You stink!"
"You stink, too!" yelled Francine. "You—hmmm . . ."

At the PTA fund-raiser, Mr. Haney introduced the band. "I am pleased to present the musical stylings of U . . ." He paused.

"STINK!" the whole band called out.

They started to play. The audience went wild.

"U Stink! U Stink! U Stink!" the crowd chanted.

The next day at school, the TV show *Almost Live* wanted to interview Francine.

"So, what's next?" asked the reporter. "Another concert? A record deal? A tour?"

"Music isn't about making money," said Francine. "U Stink will never sell out. We'd rather quit!"

After school, Francine told Fern and Binky what had happened.
"We could have been on TV!" said Fern.
"No way," said Francine. "We're not sellouts!"
The Tibble twins ran over.
"Aren't you Francine Frensky?" asked Timmy.
"Can we have your autograph?" asked Tommy.
"It's U Stink!" shouted some other kids.
Francine walked away, but the others stayed behind to sign autographs.

"Let's form our own band," said Arthur.

"It can't be that hard," said George. "It's only rock 'n' roll."

"And we could call our band *We Stink!*" said Buster.

"Perfect!" said Arthur.

Later that day, Francine saw Binky, Fern, and Molly on TV.
"What are your plans?" asked the reporter.
"Well," said Fern, "maybe we could make a CD."
"Or some action figures," Binky said.
Francine was furious. "Those traitors!"

At rehearsal, Francine was still angry about the TV interview.
"Those people want us to sell out," she said.
"It's not selling out to go on TV," said Fern.
"It is so," said Francine. "Binky, do *you* want to sell out?"
He thought for a minute. "Maybe. I need new pants."
"That's it!" Francine said. "I'm leaving U Stink! 'Cause *you stink!*"

The next morning, Mr. Haney announced that U Stink would be performing at the city library's book sale.

Francine overheard Muffy and Prunella talking about U Stink.
"What happened to Francine?" asked Muffy.
"Oh, she quit the band," Prunella said. "The *real* news is that I just got tickets to the Backstreet Boys concert!"
"My father's a sponsor," Muffy said, "so I get to go backstage!"

U STINK RULES!
HAND SOAP

Meanwhile, We Stink was having its first rehearsal.
"I hate to tell you guys," hollered D.W., "but you stink!"
"No," Arthur said. "*We* Stink. Our name is *We* Stink."
"That's what I said," D.W. answered. "You stink!"

"Arthur, can't you rehearse outside?" shouted Mom.

"We need the piano," yelled Arthur.

With Francine gone, U Stink had to rehearse at Fern's house.
"We can't keep playing the same thing over and over," said Mrs. MacGrady.
"Can anyone write music?" Molly asked. "Besides Francine?"
Mrs. MacGrady, Fern, and Binky shook their heads.

The next day, Muffy had plans to make U Stink famous.

"I'm your new manager. I've decided we'll do a video and send it to the Backstreet Boys. Then we'll go on tour with them. Then —" She stopped when she saw Francine's angry face.

"Sellout," Francine said to Fern, and stalked away.

Later that day, Francine decided to join the competition. She offered to drum for We Stink.

But they hadn't played for long before Francine stopped them.

"George, can't you sing on key?" she asked.

"What's 'on key'?" asked George.

"You guys are terrible," said Francine. "You need more players. *Good* ones."

"Hey, this is *our* band," said Buster. "If you don't think we're good enough, well . . . I quit!"

"Me, too!" said Arthur.

At the Backstreet Boys concert that night, the reporter from *Almost Live* saw U Stink waiting in line.

"What's new with U Stink?" she asked.

"Nothing — that's the problem," said Molly. "We need a new drummer, a new song . . ."

"We do not!" said Fern.

"What about *my* new song?" asked Binky.

"It hurts my ears," Molly said.

The three of them began to argue.

"Is this the end of U Stink?" said the reporter. "Stay tuned!"

Backstage, Muffy jumped into the elevator with Nick. Just as it began to move, she pushed the stop button.

"What happened?" Nick asked.

"We seem to have stopped!" said Muffy. "So let me tell you about the deal of a lifetime for you and the Boys."

She pulled down a slide screen. "It's the chance to tour with my band, U Stink! Here's how the profits look...."

The other Boys stood behind the stage curtain, waiting for Nick.
The audience was getting restless.
"Can't you go on without Nick?" Mr. Crosswire asked.
Kevin shook his head. "We need him."
"Did anyone check the elevator?" asked A.J.

Muffy answered the elevator phone. "Hi, Daddy!" she said. "No, I haven't closed the deal yet."
"The Boys need Nick to start the concert," said Mr. Crosswire. "I can't hold off the crowd forever!"
Muffy pushed the start button, but nothing happened. She pushed it again. Still nothing.
"Daddy, we really are stuck!" Muffy said. She paused. "But I have an idea."

Mr. Crosswire went to the microphone. "There's been a slight delay with the Boys, but I'd like to announce that U Stink is here, and their manager says they'd love to perform for you!"

"I can't go up there," gasped Binky. "Not without Francine."

"You have to, Binky," said Molly. "Francine?"

"We really need you, Francine," said Fern. "Will you come with us? Please?"

After a moment, Francine smiled. "All right. Let's rock!"

Onstage, Francine looked out at the huge crowd . . . and froze.

"Francine, we need a beat!" said Molly.

"Francine!" whispered Fern.

But Francine couldn't move.

Then she heard a voice in her ear. It was Brian! "Don't look at the crowd. Just think about the music."

Francine took a deep breath and started playing.

Fern began to sing. Her voice was shaky. Then Kevin's voice joined in. Then A.J. and Howie D. began to sing, too.

The Boys harmonized with U Stink and even made up a new verse. The song was better than ever!

By the end of the song, Nick had joined everyone onstage, and the crowd was cheering wildly.

U Stink got to watch the rest of the concert from backstage.

"Wow," Francine said. "They're really good."

"It's only the beginning for U Stink," Muffy said. "Today Elwood City, tomorrow the world!"

"No way," said Binky. "I don't like crowds. I have to quit."

"Me, too," said Molly. "This blister on my finger is killing me."

"And I miss playing bingo," said Mrs. MacGrady.

"But everyone loved us!" said Fern.

"Yeah!" Francine agreed. "Are you sure you guys want to quit?"

Molly, Binky, and Mrs. MacGrady all nodded.

After the show, Francine apologized to the Boys.

"I'm sorry I called you sellouts," Francine said. "You guys are really good musicians. It's okay to want fame. Just don't forget the most important part — music!"

Howie D. handed Muffy her pie chart and slides. "Very professional. You could be our manager," he joked.

"Did you hear that?" said Muffy. "Maybe in a few years I can reunite U Stink and the Backstreet Boys on tour! It's actually pretty smart for U Stink to break up — it'll create demand! It'll create buzz! It'll..."